Wilbur

Winnie the Witch

Miss Parmar

Winnie Adds Magic!

The Little Ordinaries

Miss Keen

Arthur

For Alesha Bonser—K.P.
Happy 75th birthday to my old school, Impington Village
College—xx

OXFORD
UNIVERSITY PRESS

Great Clarendon Street, Oxford OX2 6DP

Oxford University Press is a department of the University of Oxford.
It furthers the University's objective of excellence in research, scholarship,
and education by publishing worldwide in

Oxford New York

Auckland Cape Town Dar es Salaam Hong Kong Karachi
Kuala Lumpur Madrid Melbourne Mexico City Nairobi
New Delhi Shanghai Taipei Toronto

With offices in

Argentina Austria Brazil Chile Czech Republic France Greece
Guatemala Hungary Italy Japan Poland Portugal Singapore
South Korea Switzerland Thailand Turkey Ukraine Vietnam

Oxford is a registered trade mark of Oxford University Press
in the UK and in certain other countries

British Library Cataloguing in Publication Data
Data available

ISBN: 978-0-19-273666-6 (paperback)

2 4 6 8 10 9 7 5 3 1

Printed in Great Britain

Paper used in the production of this book is a natural, recyclable product
made from wood grown in sustainable forests. The manufacturing process
conforms to the environmental regulations of the country of origin.

Laura Owen and Korky Paul

Winnie
Adds Magic!

OXFORD
UNIVERSITY PRESS

contents

Winderella

Winnie Adds Magic!

Winnie Grows Her Own

'Home sweet-as-a-sweetie home!' said Winnie, skipping up the path to her front door. She and Wilbur had been staying with her sister Wendy. It had rained all week, and Wendy had been on a gherkin and grapefruit diet. 'That holiday was about as much fun as an itchy armpit,' said Winnie.

But now the sun was shining, and they were home.

'What shall we eat first, and second, and third?' asked Winnie, as she turned the key in her front door, and—**creak**—pushed it open. 'What shall we . . . oh!' A waft of stale air hit them from the damp, cold house. They put down their cases.

'Mrrow?' said Wilbur.

'We'll open the windows and it'll soon be as fresh as a dodo,' said Winnie.

Meanwhile it was warmer and nicer outside the house than in it.

'Let's make a great big feast, and eat it outside while the house airs,' said Winnie.

Wilbur opened the fridge. It was empty except for one withered cheese worm and a very disgusting smell. **Slam!** Wilbur shut the door fast.

Winnie opened the larder door—
creak!—and out flew two bats and a
beetle. The shelves and racks were bare.

'Oh, polecat petticoats!' said Winnie.
'I forgot that we emptied everything
before we went to Wendy's. We'll have to
go shopping.'

So Winnie and Wilbur went to the shop.
But the shop was, 'Shut for the holidays'.

'Oh, botherations!' wailed Winnie.
'Now what? I really fancy a picnic!' Her
tummy rumbled.

On the walk home they passed fields of cows and corn. They saw people carrying bags of food for picnics. That gave Winnie an idea.

'Get your dungarees on, Wilbur. We're going to grow our own picnic!'

11

Back in her garden, Winnie rolled
up her sleeves. 'We need butter and
cheese.' Winnie waved her wand once.
'Abradacabra!' And instantly there was a
cow.

'Moo!'

Winnie waved her wand again.
'Abradacabra!' And there was a pair of
woolly goats.

'Berrr!'

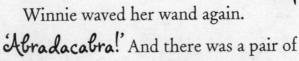

'I want salad and crisps for the picnic,'
said Winnie. She pointed her wand and
zapped. And tomato and potato and
pepper and cucumber plants appeared.

   'And we need buns and bread, so . . .'
Winnie waved and waved her wand.
'Abradacabra!'

13

There was a clucking, flapping flock of
chickens, and a patch of corn, and another
of sugar beet.

Winnie looked around at her garden
farm.

'Aah!' she breathed in the fresh country
air. Then she breathed in again and
spluttered because the cow and the goat
and the chickens had all already done
things that didn't smell lovely.

'Quick, let's get harvesting, Wilbur!'
said Winnie. 'I'll cut the corn while you
milk the giddy goats, and we'll soon be
baking bread and making pongy cheese for
sandwiches.'

Winnie bent over to cut the corn.

'Berrr!' The cross goats didn't want to be milked by Wilbur. They ran and—**butt!**—rammed into Winnie's bottom. **Weee!**—they tossed her into the air so that she fell back down—**splat!**—on a great big cowpat.

As Winnie tried to get up, she fell
onto the corn, squashing it flat. **Peck-
flutter!** Along ran the chickens to peck
at the corn but their flapping scared the
cow, who **moo-kicked** over the bucket
of milk, and trampled the tomatoes and
cucumbers.

Suddenly Winnie's farm was a mess.
Winnie was a mess. Wilbur was a mess too.

'Botheramations!' said Winnie.

She stripped off her muddy, stinky, squelchy clothes. Then she waved her wand, *Abradacabra!* And instantly her clothes were washed, and flapping on a washing line to dry.

'That's better!' she said. 'Now I need a bubble-scrubble bath to get *me* clean too!'

Winnie's big bubbly bath made her feel much better.

She went outside to fetch her dress, but
a goat was eating it. The chickens were
wearing her knickers and the cow was
trampling on her hat.

'Oh, frilly bloomers!' wailed poor
Winnie. 'I need my clothes! And my
tummy is as empty as a deflated balloon,
and there's nothing to eat! It's not *fair!*'

She stamped her foot, but it stamped on an egg that a chicken had just laid—**crack-splat!**

'And now I can't even eat that!'

Winnie closed her eyes, and for a long horrible moment, Wilbur thought that she was about to burst into tears. So Wilbur thought fast, and then he acted fast. Moving so fast that he was just a blur, clever Wilbur made everything all right.

He sheered the goats—**buzz!**—and knitted—**clickety-click!**—their wool into a hairy-scary brown onesie for Winnie to wear. He even decorated it with feathers from the chickens.

'Oo, thank you, Wilbur!' said Winnie,
pulling it on. 'That's as cosy as a bug in a
rug in a snug hug, that is!'

Then Wilbur plucked—**squawk!**—a
quill from a chicken, and he wrote a big
sign that said, 'See the rare Winniebeast.
Please *do* feed the animal!'

'Meeow!' he said to make the
Winniebeast stand behind the sign.

And suddenly people walking past with
their picnics stopped and stared. Then
they held out cakes and sandwiches and
drinks for the Winniebeast to eat.

23

'**Mmm-yum!**' said the strange Winniebeast, and she passed some of the food on to the cat that seemed to live on the garden farm with her.

All afternoon Winnie and Wilbur scoffed buns and baguettes and pies and pasties.

By the time the sun was sinking in the sky, Winnie and Wilbur were as full as a bull in a china shop who likes eating china.

'Cock-a-doodle-moo!' called Winnie appreciatively to the last person to give her a bit of picnic.

PLE

As it got dark, the picnickers headed home, and so did Winnie and Wilbur. The house was nicely aired now.

'And do you know what, Wilbur?' said Winnie. 'I'm actually-pactually glad there's no food in the house because I know that I won't be hungry again for at least a week!'

The onesie was nicely loose on a fat
tummy, and Winnie didn't even need
to change into her nightie for bed. And
Wilbur found that the hairy Winniebeast
was lovely and soft and warm to sleep on.

Winnie's Treasure Hunt

It was a sunny day, and Winnie and
Wilbur were skipping. Wilbur could
twiddle his rope above his head and below
his feet between each jump. Winnie needed
a rhyme to help her rhythm.

'One—**hop**—maggot, two—**hop**—
maggots, three—**hop**—maggots, four.
Five maggots, six maggots, seven maggots
more! Dropping those maggots all over
the floor, what the knitted noodles am I
skipping for?'

Sigh! 'I'll tell you what I'm skipping for, Wilbur. I'm skipping like a kangaroo with fleas because I'm as bored as a cheese board that only ever has cheddar on it. Why can't something interesting happen around here?'

Just as Winnie said that, a man with an eye patch and a wooden leg walked past. He was looking intently at the ground. Hmm, thought Winnie. *He* looks interesting.

'Excuse me!' said Winnie. 'Are you a pirate?'

'Arr!' said the man. 'Good arrfternoon, Marrm! Indeed I arr a pirate, and my name's Arrthur.'

30

'Are you a mean sort of a pirate who might kidnap a witch or a cat?'

'Ha harr!' said Arthur, swivelling his one good eye.

Hiss-spit! went Wilbur, and Winnie took a step back.

But then Arthur sort of sagged. 'Er,
no. I ain't like that really,' he said. 'That's
what people generally suppose I'm like.
That's why nobody likes me. But the truth
is, I be a quiet sort of a chap who just
wants to find the treasure on this map. I've
been searchin' and searchin' for a big X
what marrks the spot where the treasure
be, but I just can't find it.'

'Would you like Wilbur and me to help
you?' said Winnie.

33

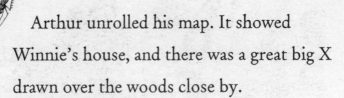

Arthur unrolled his map. It showed
Winnie's house, and there was a great big X
drawn over the woods close by.

'I've been all overr that wood,' said
Arthur. 'But I couldn't see an X anywhere.'

'That's because you need to look down
on the *whole* wood,' said Winnie. 'Then it
would look like the map.'

'But flyin' ain't possible unless you be a
parrot!' said Arthur.

'Yes, it witchy-well is . . .' said Winnie,
'on my broom!'

Arthur hardly dared to look out of his one
good eye as the broom zoomed upwards.

'There's the X!' said Winnie, pointing at
two paths that crossed to make a big clear X.

'So I was standing right on top of it!'
laughed Arthur. 'Can we go down and get
digging now?'

Arthur had a spade in his pack, but
Winnie was too impatient for spade
digging. She waved her wand.
'Abradacabra!'

And instantly there was a shiny yellow
digger that she climbed into, and soon—
brooooom-clunk-heave!—she was
digging a hole in the middle of the wood.

'I can see the treasure chest!' said
Arthur, dancing with excitement. 'There it
is at larrst!'

They all dug to get the chest out of
the ground, and then Arthur lifted the
lid—**Creak! Sparkle! Twinkle!
Chink!**—there was a huge hoard of
jewels and coins and more.

'Whoopy-do!' said Winnie, putting
on sunglasses because the treasure was so
bright. They were all soon trying on crowns
and necklaces, and juggling with gems.

'It's been my life's work, to find this treasure,' said Arthur, and he suddenly stopped playing with it, and stood still. He scratched his head. 'And now I've got it, I, er, ain't quite sure what to do with it, to be honest with you.'

Arthur bent down and tried to pick
up the treasure chest. **Grunt-heave!**
It didn't move. 'That's awful heavy,' he said.
'I left my ship in a harrbour forty-three year
ago, and it's a long way off from here.'

'That treasure would be too heavy for
my broom to carry,' said Winnie. 'Perhaps
you should take it by cart.'

'A carrt would do it!' said Arthur, brightening. 'Oh, but then I'd have to guarrd the cart. Otherwise that treasure might be stolen.'

'Good if it was!' said Winnie. 'Then you wouldn't have the bother guarding it anymore.'

'Well, that be true,' said Arthur. 'Except then what would I do with myself?'

'Play with your friends! Do your hobbies!' said Winnie.

'Ain't got no friends nor hobbies,' said Arthur. 'Oh, dear. I don't know what to do.'

'Well, I do,' said Winnie.

'What be that, then?' said Arthur.

'Have a treasure-hunt party!' said Winnie. 'Invite everyone, and then they will be your new friends!'

'I've never had a parrty afore,' said Arthur. 'But it would be nice to have friends at larrst!'

So Winnie got busy with her wand. Swish! 'Abradacabra!'

43

Instantly the wood was decorated, and
there was a table full of food. **Swish!**
'*Abradacabra!*' Invitations flew off to all
Winnie's friends and relations.

Then Winnie and Wilbur and Arthur hid bits of treasure here, there, and everywhere, and they made up treasure-hunt clues about where each thing was.

'Wilbur, write down "Under something that is over something clever",' said Winnie.

'Meow?' said Wilbur, but he did it.

Arthur wrote, 'A strange new fruit in a tree.' They did clues for every bit of treasure.

And then the guests arrived.

Everyone enjoyed the party very much.

After all, who wouldn't enjoy a treasure

hunt with a pirate?

Jerry found a crown that he could wear
as a bracelet. Mrs Parmar looked delightful
in diamonds. They all ate lots, and chatted
more, and at the end of it Arthur said,
'I likes parrties!'

Then he wiped away a tear. 'I likes friends too.' **Sniff!** He blew his nose on a big piratical hanky. 'You really are magic, Winnie, giving me friends.'

'It wasn't magic that gave you friends, you silly old pirate. It was you!' said Winnie.

48

'Now, stop being as soppy as a soggy
flannel! I'll fly you home to your ship.
Wilbur would like a squidoctopus for his
tea, fresh from the sea, and I'd like a paddle!'

Wilbur got his fresh squidoctopus. And
Winnie taught Arthur a hobby: skipping
with the ropes on board his ship. **Skip-
bump-skip-bump!** went the real and
wooden legs. He was surprisingly good at
skipping.

'Oh, gnats' kneecaps!' said Winnie, when they got back home. 'I meant to take one sparkly-twinkly bit for myself to remind me of a day when something interesting *did* happen, but I forgot to find one.'

But when Winnie took off her hat at bedtime, she found that she *did* have a bit of treasure after all. Nobody had guessed that 'under something that is over something really clever' could possibly mean her hat!

Winderella

'Meeeow!' **Bang!**

'What the elephant's elbow was that?' wondered Winnie, suddenly sitting up in bed.

'Wilbur?' said Winnie. 'Is that you?'

At first, there was no reply. Then a 'Meeeow!' downstairs. The noise seemed to be coming from the kitchen. As sneakily as a spy spider, Winnie crept down the stairs, and quietly pushed open the kitchen door to find . . .

53

Wilbur waving Winnie's wand at his food bowl, and muttering strange kinds of meows.

'Are you trying to magic yourself some breakfast, Wilbur?'

Wilbur jumped into the air, hid the wand behind his back, shook his head, 'Mrro.'

'Yes, you wobbly-well were!' laughed Winnie. 'But cats can't *Abradacabra!* you know! So it won't work. Give the wand to me, and *I'll* magic you a mega-mousey-fishy breakfast.'

Winnie was just reaching for the wand when,

Bleepety-bloop. Bleepety-bloop!

'That's my mobile moan,' said Winnie, delving into her pocket. 'Hello? Oh, hello Mrs Parmar! Yes. Yes. Yes. No trouble at all. Don't you worry, Mrs P. I'll be with you in one shake of a bat's bottom. Oo, and I've got my own broom, so that's perfect, isn't it? Bye!'

'Meow?' asked Wilbur.

'That was Mrs Parmar from the school,'
said Winnie. 'It's their panto tonight—
Cinderella—but the little ordinaries have
all gone down with chicken-licken pox,
so *they* can't do the show. They need
someone to step into Cinderella's shoes
because they've sold lots of tickets, and
so the show must go on. Oo, I've always
wanted to be an actress. This is a dream
come true!'

'Meow?' said Wilbur.

Poor Wilbur. *He'd* always wanted to be able to do magic, and now he very much wanted breakfast, but neither of these dreams looked as though *they* would come true today.

Winnie and Wilbur flew to the school, straight in through a window.

'I didn't park the broom outside because it's the perfect prop for Cinderella. Or Winderella, as she will be now!' said Winnie.

'Oh, but I'd thought that I . . .' began Mrs Parmar, who happened to be wearing a dress with patches all over it, and she had soot on her face.

'. . . that you'd like to be Prince
Charming?' said Winnie. 'Good idea! And
my cousin Cuthbert can be Aladdin . . .'

'But there *is* no Aladdin in the story of
Cinderella!' wailed Mrs Parmar.

'Maybe not,' said Winnie. 'But there *is*
Aladdin in the story of Winderella. There's
a beanstalk too.'

'A *beanstalk*!' Mrs Parmar had gone
pale. 'Why would there . . .'

'So that we can have the giant, of course,' said Winnie. 'My neighbour Jerry can be the giant.'

'Oh,' said Mrs Parmar weakly.

Jerry had to bend down to fit into the school hall. But his carpentry skills were very useful in making scenery.

Bang! Crash! Shatter!

'Oh dear,' said Mrs Parmar.

'Good news, Mrs P,' said Winnie. 'I've got three *really* ugly sisters, so we'll have three instead of two.' And she pulled out her mobile moan, and rang Wanda and Wilma and Wendy.

'Dear, oh, dear,' said Mrs Parmar.

'Get your britches on, Mrs P,'
said Winnie. She waved her wand.
'*Abradacabra!*' And Mrs Parmar was
instantly Prince Charm-ar.

'Oo,' said Winnie with a big smile, 'and
I've got a brillaramaroodles idea for who
can be my Fairy Godmother!'

'Really?' said Prince Charm-ar. But she
didn't dare ask who that might be.

They'd only just sorted out all the costumes and scenery before the audience began to arrive, so nobody quite knew how the story would work out.

Swish! went the velvet curtains, and there was Winderella, sweeping the sooty hearth, and weeping.

'Oh, poor 'iccle me!' wailed Winderella. 'Here I am doing all the work, and three blooming ugly big sisters bossing me around all the time!'

'Oi, you didn't say we were *ugly* sisters when you asked us to be in your panto!' said a furious Wanda, wig wobbling as she stormed in from the wings. And soon Wendy, Wilma, and Wanda were chasing Winderella all over the stage.

So Winderella got onto her broomstick, and flew above the set.

'Yay!' cheered the audience.

Then the ugly sisters gave chase on *their* broomsticks until Wilma got caught in the beanstalk, and Jerry had to rescue her.

'Bravo!' everyone shouted.

'Well,' said Prince Charm-ar. 'They do seem to be enjoying the show!' She looked almost charming with relief.

It came to the moment when Winderella
needed to get ready to go to the ball.

There was a slight pause.

'Ahem!' said Winderella. 'If only my
dear old Furry Godmother would arrive!'
Winderella was beckoning frantically to
the side of the stage.

 And on twirled Wilbur, pretty as a pansy, in a pink tutu and matching petal wings, and waving a star-topped wand that dropped sparkling glitter all around.

'Ahh!' said the audience.

'Can you magic me a ball gown, please, Furry Godmother?' said Winderella. 'A gown so glorious that I *can* go to the ball?'

And the Furry Godmother waved his
wand at Winderella and said, 'Meeow!'

At exactly that same moment
Winderella sneakily twirled her wooden
spoon that looked strangely like a wand,
and did a little cough that sounded
strangely like,

'Ab-*cough*-ra-*cough*-dacabra!'

Winderella was magically whirled into
the most beautiful ball gown that anyone
had ever seen. And the Furry Godmother
was gazing at his starry wand with his
mouth wide open in astonishment.

'Hooray!' everyone cheered.

After that the plot of the panto became even more strange. But it all ended with a jolly dance finale, until Jerry the Giant fell straight through the stage floor. Cousin 'Aladdin' Cuthbert threw sweets for everyone so they didn't mind about not understanding the show.

The audience clapped and clapped.

'Thank you, Winnie!' sighed Prince Charm-ar.

Wilbur took off his tutu and wings,
but he refused to give back the sparkly
star wand. Back home, when Winnie went
to the cupboard to find his favourite tin
of spicy minced mice for a very, very
late breakfast, Wilbur put a paw on her
arm to hold her back. Then he closed
his eyes tight, waved his wand, and
shouted, 'Meow!'

It was lucky that he *did* have his eyes closed because it gave Winnie just enough time to slip the food into his bowl before hiding the tin behind her back. Wilbur was *amazed*.

So *both* their dreams had come true!

Winnie Adds Magic!

The children were in the middle of a maths lesson at the school when . . .

'Yoo hoo snail goo!' Winnie the Witch was at the classroom window. She looked scary with her face pressed against the glass.

'Aarrgghhh!' yelled the children, leaping up and running for the door . . . where they bounced off Mrs Parmar, coming in.

'Winnie, come in through the door, please,' said Mrs Parmar. 'Do sit down, children, and carry on with your lesson.'

'Add one to one, and what do you get?' asked the maths teacher, Miss Keen. She pointed at some pictures. 'If you had one cat and one mouse, how many animals would you have altogether?'

'Two!' shouted the children.

'That's not blooming right!' said
Winnie, knocking her hat off as she came
through the doorway. Wilbur, at her
ankles, had something pink and stringy
hanging from his mouth.

'It most certainly *is* right!' said Miss
Keen. 'One add one is two. It always has
been and always will be!'

'Not if it's a cat and a mouse,' said
Winnie. 'Wilbur just added a mouse
to himself, and altogether there is now
just ...' Winnie pointed at Wilbur, 'one
cat. One plus one equals one, see?'

'Well I've never heard such ...!' puffed
Miss Keen.

'Never mind sums,' said Mrs Parmar. 'Children, Winnie is here because she has kindly agreed to look after our class goldfish over half term.'

'But . . . but . . . won't one witch plus one cat plus one fish add up to just two?' asked Micky, looking doubtfully at Wilbur as he slurped up the last of the mouse tail.

'Your fish will be quite safe with me,' said Winnie. 'What's his name?'

F is gh as in 'cough'
I is o as in 'women'
sh is ti as in 'addition'

Fish — Ghoti

'It's Ghoti, pronounced "Goa-tee",' said Mrs Parmar, 'but it actually spells "fish" because it's *gh* as in "cou*gh*", *o* as in "w*o*men", and *ti* as in "addi*ti*on".'

'Oh,' said Winnie doubtfully. Perhaps the little ordinaries had as much to learn about spelling as they did about sums?

80

She picked up the goldfish bowl and took a step towards the door. She hadn't noticed her hat on the floor, and … **trip, crash** … Ghoti the fish went flying through the air, coming down to land just where Wilbur was 'yawning' widely.

'Noooo!' shouted the children. 'Abradacabra!'

Quick as a lick Winnie waved her wand, and Ghoti's fins flapped like wings, and he flew beyond Wilbur to land in Miss Keen's mug of tea.

'There,' said Winnie. 'No harm done.' Except that Miss Keen was just about to take a sip . . .

'Noooo!' shouted the children again.

'*Abradacabra!*' Winnie waved her
wand at the mug . . . which instantly
turned into a giant, see-through mug
goldfish bowl. 'Perfectamundo!' said
Winnie. 'A bowl with a handle. Come on,
Wilbur, let's take him home.'

Back home, Winnie put down Ghoti's bowl.

'Fish like flies' eggs to eat,' said Winnie, and she sprinkled some into the water for Ghoti, then licked her fingers. 'Mm, yummy!'

'Meow?' asked Wilbur.

'Oh, I'll feed you in a minute,' said
Winnie. 'I just need to make sure that dear
little Ghoti is properly settled first.' Winnie
found toys to put in the fish bowl, and she
took photos. Wilbur's tummy rumbled.

'Meeeow!' he wailed, and he put a paw
into the fish bowl, tempted by that fat
juicy fish.

'Leave him alone!' said Winnie. 'How could I face the little ordinaries if you'd scoffed their pet?'

So Wilbur tried to ignore his hunger and the tempting fish. But, whenever Winnie wasn't looking, Ghoti made faces at Wilbur. Then he swam backwards to show his bottom to Wilbur.

'Mrrow!' Wilbur prepared to pounce . . .
and Winnie grabbed him.

Slam!

Wilbur was out in the rain, with the
door shut tight.

'Poor 'iccle fishy-wishy,' said Winnie,
and she gave Ghoti some ants' eggs and
some mini maggots. She made him an
underwater playground out of some bones
and bits. And Wilbur watched her through
the window.

That window was a little bit open.
When Winnie fell asleep on the sofa
Wilbur found a long skinny stick and
a piece of string. He dug up a squiggly,
wiggly worm. Then he tied the worm to
the string, and the string to the stick.

'Me-he-he!' chuckled Wilbur.

Snore went Winnie as Wilbur posted his worm and string and stick through the window and dangled it over Ghoti's bowl.

Ghoti grabbed the dangling worm and Wilbur licked his lips as Ghoti came closer and closer . . . but then he fell . . . right into Winnie's snoring open mouth!

Gulp! Cough!

Winnie spluttered and sent Ghoti
flying, back into his bowl.

'Wilbur!' roared Winnie. 'You are in
big trouble!' She stormed outside. But
Wilbur looked so wet and hungry that
Winnie instantly took pity.

'Oh, Wilbur, you're a soggy, sad moggy,
and I still haven't fed you! Come back
inside and let's be friends again?'

Ghoti was showing off in his bowl,
pretending to be a leaping dolphin.

Grrrr! went Wilbur, his paw twitching.

'I agree, Wilbur!' said Winnie. 'That fish
is annoying! Out you go, Ghoti the fish!'

Winnie and Wilbur stomped back
outside and emptied the fish bowl into the
pond.

'You can stay there until we take you back to school,' said Winnie. Ghoti flipped onto his back and did a fancy backstroke to show off.

'We're not impressed,' said Winnie, turning her back. She didn't see something else that was impressed by Ghoti's swimming display.

It rained all half term, so Winnie and Wilbur stayed indoors playing dafts and snappy families. They forgot all about Ghoti until . . .

'Winnie!' said Mrs Parmar on the telling moan. 'You haven't forgotten to bring Ghoti back to school today, have you? Er, he *is* all right, isn't he? The children are a bit worried.'

'Oh, he's as fine as a tooth comb!' said Winnie, but she had her fingers and toes crossed as she said it.

Winnie and Wilbur rushed into the garden and tried to fish Ghoti out with his bowl, but they couldn't catch him. So Winnie waved her wand and instantly it became a fishing rod, and the gnomes around the pond began fishing, too. Did they catch Ghoti? They certainly did. *And* they caught the 'something else' from the pond *and* eleven little baby fish too!

'Too many for one fish bowl!' said
Winnie. So she waved her fishing-rod
wand to make a proper family-sized bowl.

The children thought that the baby fish
were magic.

'A baby fish each!' said Winnie.

'But how did . . . ?' began Miss Keen.

'Well, there was one fish plus one fish,
and that *didn't* make two fish, did it?'
said Winnie. 'See? You shouldn't really be
teaching sums, should you!'

Enjoy more magic moments
with Winnie the Witch!